ROSE COMES TO AMERICA

by Linda Cernak
illustrated by Joanne Renaud

Harcourt
SCHOOL PUBLISHERS

Requests for permission to make copies of any part of the work should be addressed to School Permissions and Copyrights, Harcourt, Inc., 6277 Sea Harbor Drive, Orlando, Florida 32887-6777. Fax: 407-345-2418.

HARCOURT and the Harcourt Logo are trademarks of Harcourt, Inc., registered in the United States of America and/or other jurisdictions.

Printed in China

ISBN 10: 0-15-351537-6
ISBN 13: 978-0-15-351537-8

Ordering Options
ISBN 10: 0-15-351214-8 (Grade 4 Advanced Collection)
ISBN 13: 978-0-15-351214-8 (Grade 4 Advanced Collection)
ISBN 10: 0-15-358127-1 (package of 5)
ISBN 13: 978-0-15-358127-4 (package of 5)

4 5 6 7 8 9 10 0940 12 11 10 09

Lauren's grandma lived just down the block, so Lauren often spent the afternoon at her grandmother's apartment. One rainy afternoon, Lauren was looking for a book to read in Grandma's bookcase. As she was looking, she noticed an old, dusty scrapbook stuck between *Tom Sawyer* and *The Adventures of Huckleberry Finn.*

Grandma took the album down and said, "That is the story of how your great-grandmother came to this country. I haven't looked at this album in years! Would you like to take a look?"

"Oh, yes, Grandma," Lauren said excitedly. She jumped up on the couch and snuggled next to her grandmother. She loved to hear stories about people from the past. Grandma opened the scrapbook. It was a collection of postcards, letters, and some very old photographs.

"A long time ago," said Grandma, "back at the beginning of this century, a young girl lived in a country called Italy."

Grandma got up, pulled out an atlas, and opened it up to a map of Italy. "Italy is shaped like a very long boot, and it even has a heel and a toe." Grandma pointed to the toe part. "Now that is where your great-grandmother, Rose Gallo, came from. She was married to a young man named Dominic Gallo. It was Dominic who wanted to come to America. He knew that there were many good opportunities here for work."

"Did they fly here?" asked Lauren.

Grandma chuckled and replied, "No, in those days, people came by ship."

"Your great-grandmother came to this country in 1923, when she was twenty-one years old. She had a baby boy who was two years old."

"That sure was a long time ago!" exclaimed Lauren, "They didn't even have TV back then, did they?"

"No, they didn't," said Grandma, "but they learned about other places by reading newspapers and books, and by talking to other people. Dominic knew about America because his brother had come here two years earlier, in 1921. His brother wrote him letters describing what it was like in this country. He told Dominic about his family and what he did for work."

Carefully, Grandma opened the scrapbook. There on the first page was an old letter. It had been placed inside a plastic sleeve to protect it and to keep it from crumbling.

Grandma read the letter to Lauren:

Dear Dominic,

We are living in a place called Brooklyn. It is a part of the city of New York. All the buildings here are so big. I work at the shipyard making seventy-three cents an hour. The work is hard, but the money is good. Every night I take an underground train called a subway home. On weekends, we take the subway to a place called Coney Island. I have sent you a postcard of Coney Island to show to Rose. Life is very good here in America. I hope to see you soon.

Your brother, Angelo.

Lauren studied the postcard. "I've been to Coney Island once, but it sure didn't look like this!" she exclaimed.

"Times change," replied Grandma. "In those days, seventy-three cents bought a lot of things, too."

"Then what happened?" asked Lauren.

"Your great-grandfather arranged for passage for himself on a steamship. He wanted to find work first, and then he would send for your great-grandmother and their little boy. The journey was an extremely long one. Thousands of people from all over Europe came to America during that time," said Grandma.

"Your great-grandfather was a stonemason by trade, which means he made buildings of stone. When he came to America, he began working in the shipyard with his brother. He worked hard for weeks, and then he found a small apartment right here in Brooklyn. It was time to send for Rose and their boy."

Grandma flipped through the pages of the scrapbook and found an old photo, brown with age, of Great-grandpa and his brother. "When it was time for Rose and her little son, Joseph, to come to America, Rose became very sad. She knew it would be a very long time before she would see her family again. She left behind her mother, father, three sisters, and a brother, and she also had to say good-bye to many friends."

Grandma continued her story. "On the day Rose left, she boarded the great steamship with two thousand other passengers. These people, who left their own countries to travel to America, were called immigrants. Your great-grandmother told me a kind lady saw her crying and comforted her that day."

"The voyage across the sea was difficult. Many people slept in tiny little cabins that had anywhere from four to six bunks. There was very little room to move around, and it was extremely hot and crowded," said Grandma.

"At mealtime, your great-grandmother and her little boy would go to a dining room with a long table and eat with other passengers. Many of the ships that came from Italy served foods like pasta and bread. Most other immigrants were served meals of potatoes, soup, and meat."

"Great-grandmother must have been very brave to make such a long trip," said Lauren.

"Yes, she certainly was," said Grandma. "She was coming to a strange land where she didn't know anyone except for her husband and his brother, and she didn't speak English either."

9

"What happened next, Grandma?" asked Lauren.

"Well, the voyage across the ocean took many days. The day that Rose finally arrived in New York was very exciting for all of the passengers on board. From very far away, they could see the Statue of Liberty. I remember clearly your great-grandmother telling me that she burst into tears when she saw the statue. 'It was so magnificent,' she said, 'but I did not expect her to be green!' She could not believe all the boats in the harbor either. The passengers all stood huddled together on deck, waiting to see what would happen next," said Grandma.

Grandma took an old photo out of the
scrapbook. "That's a place called Ellis Island," said
Grandma. "It was the first stop for all immigrants
when they arrived in this country. At that time,
there were so many immigrants coming into
America that they all had to go to this place first.
There were many, many ships in the harbor, and
on a single day, there might be several thousand
people coming into New York."

Grandma continued, "Rose and her little boy
waited for a long time before they finally were
allowed to get off of the steamship. Then they were
loaded onto a small boat that took them from the
steamship to the dock at Ellis Island. They went
into the large building and into a great hall called
the Registry Room. There were long lines of people
waiting to get checked into America."

"There was a lot of confusion. Inspectors put numbered tags on all of the people, and doctors checked them to make sure they didn't have any serious illnesses or diseases. It took several hours for Rose and little Joseph to go through all the checkpoints at Ellis Island. At the very end, they were sent to a special room where they had to wait for your great-grandfather to come and claim them. Women traveling alone or those who had children were not allowed to leave Ellis Island until a relative came for them," continued Grandma.

"Finally, Dominic Gallo came for his wife and child. Your great-grandmother told me that when he recognized her, his face lit up like fireworks in the night sky."

"Your great-grandfather brought his wife and child home to Brooklyn. That's where my four brothers and three sisters and I were born. Later on, when we were all grown, Rose and Dominic moved to the country, and Dominic built a lovely stone house. I stayed here in the city, and I married your grandfather."

"Did Great-grandmother ever see her family in Italy again?" wondered Lauren.

"No, I don't believe she did, but that's how it was in those days. I think it made her very sad, but she had a wonderful family right here in America."

"Do immigrants still come through Ellis Island?" asked Lauren.

"No, today Ellis Island is a museum that people can visit," said Grandma.

"Can we go there, please?" asked Lauren.

"I think that's a marvelous idea," smiled Grandma.

The very next weekend, Lauren, her father, and her grandmother took the trip out to Ellis Island. Just like the immigrants had in the past, they took a boat through the harbor and got off at the island. They walked into the large building that Rose and Dominic Gallo had passed through over eighty years ago.

"Many of the people who live in America today are the grandchildren and great-grandchildren of the immigrants who passed through these doors," said Lauren's father. "You know, it's possible we might still have some distant cousins in Italy."

"I think someday I will go back to Italy and find my relatives," said Lauren. "I think I'll fly, though."

Grandma and her father burst out laughing. "Let us go with you!" they said.

"It's a deal!" Lauren said.

Think Critically

1. If you could ask Rose a question, what would you ask her?

2. Why did Dominic and Rose want to come to America?

3. What is the main setting of the story?

4. What kind of hardships do you think immigrants faced when they arrived in this country during the 1920s?

5. How would you feel if your family left America to go live in another country?

 Social Studies

Write a Letter Think about where you would live if you could choose any place in the world. Find out about that place. Then write a letter telling a friend about your new home.

School-Home Connection Tell family members the story of Rose. Then talk about the kinds of things someone new to America would have to learn about in your town.

Word Count: 1,548

GRADE 4
Lesson 22
WORD COUNT
1,548
GENRE
Diary
LEVEL
See TG or go Online

Go online Harcourt Leveled
Readers Online Database

ISBN-13: 978-0-15-351537-8
ISBN-10: 0-15-351537-6

9 780153 515378

90000

Harcourt
SCHOOL PUBLISHERS

The Gift of Writing

by Kana Riley
illustrated by
Yvonne Buchanan